Clara Barton:
Angel of the Battlefield

CHARACTERS

Dad

Tammy

David

Clara Barton

Eliza

Glen

SETTING

North Oxford, Massachusetts, 1833
Washington, D.C., 1865
Galveston, Texas, during
the Flood of 1900

Dad: Tammy, I'm so glad you and Tommy have vacation this week. Your mother and I both have to finish writing our books. You can help me with my research.

Tammy: I always like to go on *When Machine* trips with you, Dad! And I'm really excited to be learning about Clara Barton.

Dad: While you're with me learning about Clara Barton, Mom and Tommy are in Europe interviewing Florence Nightingale. She, too, was a famous nurse.

Tammy: Clara Barton was a nurse during the Civil War, right? People called her the "Angel of the Battlefield."

Dad: That's true. But she did a lot more than that to help people. I'm most interested in how she helped found the American Red Cross. Why don't we start there with our interviews?

Tammy: But Dad, I want to find out what Clara was like when she was my age. Before she grew up and became famous.

Dad: OK, then. Let's start on her family farm in North Oxford, Massachusetts. Please set the *When Machine* to 1833.

Tammy: Great, Dad. It's all set. What will we find there?

Dad: Although Clara is only 11, she's already taking care of people. A few weeks ago, her brother David fell from a roof and hurt himself. Let's see how he's doing.

Tammy: Here we are in 1833!

Dad: And there are Clara and David.

David: Thanks, Clara, for bringing me out here to enjoy the sunshine.

Clara: I'm glad you're feeling a little better, David.

Dad: Hello, children. How are you?

David: Hello. Who are you? Where did you come from?

Dad: We just arrived from the future. This is called a *When Machine*. It can transport us to any time and any place we set it to. We want to talk with you for a few minutes.

David: That's so exciting! I'd love to travel in time. I'm David, and this is my sister Clara. Why do you want to talk with us?

Tammy: My dad is writing a book about the past. With our machine, we can visit people from other times. Clara, you're doing a really good job of taking care of your brother.

Clara: Thank you.

David: You'll have to forgive my sister. She's an amazing nurse, but she's very shy, especially around strangers.

Dad: It takes a special person to care for people the way Clara does.

David: I know. She helps me with everything. She's promised to take care of me until I'm well. How's that for a sister?

Tammy: Clara, are you thinking about becoming a nurse when you grow up?

Clara: My father wants me to become a teacher.

David: She's very smart and has been reading since she was 4. But I think she should become a nurse. She's so kind to everyone.

Dad: You're right, David. But Clara will find that out for herself. Well, we have to go. Feel better, David. And enjoy this beautiful day. Good-bye, children!

Clara and **David:** Good-bye!

Tammy: Dad, Clara hardly said anything.

Dad: I know, Tammy. I have read that she was painfully shy as a child. But as a woman she wasn't afraid of anything. I want to see how she changed. I'm setting the *When Machine* for 1865. Let's visit her then.

Tammy: Did David get better?

Dad: Yes, he did. Clara nursed him for two years while he recovered from the injury.

Tammy: How wonderful of her to take such good care of him! Here we are in 1865. This looks like Washington, D.C. Why are we here? This isn't a hospital.

Dad: No. The Civil War just ended. I want to find out about Clara's work after the war. Clara was a nurse during the war, but after the war she did important work for the government. This must be one of Clara's assistants.

Eliza: Hello. May I help you?

Tammy: Where are we?

Eliza: This is the Bureau of Records. It's run by Miss Clara Barton. Who are you?

Tammy: We're from the future. My name is Tammy. My dad is writing a book about Miss Barton. Could you tell us what you're doing here?

Eliza: The future? How strange! Well, now that the war is over, it's our job to search for men missing in action and bring them back to their families. President Lincoln was extremely impressed by the way in which Miss Barton helped the men on the battlefields. He appointed her to this job.

Tammy: How is the work going?

Eliza: Why don't you ask Miss Barton?

Clara: The work is going slowly. There were so many lives torn apart by this war. But who are you? You both look very familiar.

Dad: We met a long time ago, when you were much younger. But now I want to ask you about your work.

Clara: I have very little time. There are so many families who want to know what happened to their fathers and sons and husbands.

Tammy: You were a nurse during the Civil War. Why are you doing this now?

Clara: Ever since I was a child, I've wanted to help people who were hurt or sick. My brother David was one of the first. Now I'm trying to help families who were hurt by this terrible war.

Tammy: Weren't you very shy? I remember that from when we met many years ago.

Clara: Yes, I was.

Eliza: I never knew you as a shy person. As I recall, you started out teaching school. Wasn't that a difficult job for a shy person?

Clara: Yes, it was. But through teaching I was able to overcome my shyness. And I was never shy about helping other people.

Dad: You spend a lot of your time now speaking about your Civil War experiences, right?

Eliza: Miss Barton speaks in public all the time. And a shy person couldn't organize all this! She's had to fight for everything we've done.

Clara: I hardly remember that shy person anymore myself, Eliza. I don't want to be rude, but I must go back to work. Good-bye. I hope to see you again some day.

Dad: You will, Miss Barton. Good-bye. And thank you!

Tammy: Did she find a lot of the missing soldiers, Dad?

Dad: Yes, she found more than 20,000 of them!

Tammy: Wow! What a fantastic person. The *When Machine* is already set to 1900. Are we going to see Clara Barton there? She must have been very old by then.

Dad: She'll be there—still doing wonderful work after all those years. And here we are! This is Galveston, Texas. There's a huge flood here. Clara Barton had founded the American Red Cross almost 20 years before. And she's still running it.

Glen: Hello. What are you doing here?

Tammy: We're here to talk with Clara Barton.

Glen: Well, you've come at a bad time. The flood has caused a great deal of damage.

Dad: Can we help?

Glen: You can pile some of these sandbags over there against the riverbanks.

Clara: Glen, I'm glad to see you've got some helpers. The wind is just beginning to die down. It will take the floodwaters with it, I hope.

Tammy: Hello, Miss Barton. I am so happy to see you again.

Clara: Hello, young lady. Thank you for coming to help us. But look around you. There isn't much time for chatter.

Dad: We understand, Miss Barton. I'm writing a book about you. We've come a long way and just want a few minutes.

Clara: Well, I'm flattered. But I'm also tired. At my age, this work gets harder and harder. But there's always so much to be done. I can't just give up, can I?

Glen: The American Red Cross goes where it's needed in war and peace. That's not the way the Red Cross used to be, before Miss Barton was involved.

Tammy: But I thought you founded the Red Cross, Miss Barton.

Clara: The Red Cross started in Europe. I went there to learn about their work. I went to the battlefields of the Franco-Prussian War. The Red Cross was the first to help soldiers no matter which side they were fighting on. When I returned, I started the American Red Cross.

Glen: Miss Barton thought there was important work to do in peacetime as well.

Clara: People need help no matter what type of disaster strikes—earthquakes, fires, or floods like this one.

Glen: Excuse me, Miss Barton, but they need you on the other side of town to organize food supplies.

Clara: I must go. Good-bye, now.

Tammy and **Dad:** Thank you Miss Barton. And good-bye once again.

Tammy: Dad, this was so much fun! The *When Machine* is awesome! I've learned so much!

Dad: I've learned a lot, too. Talking with a real person helps a story come to life. The notes from our interviews will make a great book.

Tammy: I'm inspired by Clara Barton's work. Teaching, nursing, founding the American Red Cross. Helping so many people her whole life.

Dad: She truly was the "Angel of the Battlefield," and so much more. You know, Clara Barton's American Red Cross is still hard at work today, helping people in need across America and around the world. Speaking of the present, look at the time! We need to get back.

Tammy: You're right. I can hardly wait until our next *When Machine* adventure!

The End